Each Puffin Easy-to-Read book has a color-coded reading level to make book selection easy for parents and children. Because all children are unique in their reading development, Puffin's three levels make it easy for teachers and parents to find the right book to suit each individual child's reading readiness.

Level 1: Short, simple sentences full of word repetition—plus clear visual clues to help children take the first important steps toward reading.

Level 2: More words and longer sentences for children just beginning to read on their own.

Level 3: Lively, fast-paced text—perfect for children who are reading on their own.

"Readers aren't born, they're made. Desire is planted—planted by parents who work at it."

—**Jim Trelease**, author of
The Read-Aloud Handbook

For Emma

PUFFIN BOOKS
Published by the Penguin Group
Penguin Books USA Inc., 375 Hudson Street, New York, New York 10014, U.S.A.
Penguin Books Ltd, 27 Wrights Lane, London W8 5TZ, England
Penguin Books Australia Ltd, Ringwood, Victoria, Australia
Penguin Books Canada Ltd, 10 Alcorn Avenue, Toronto, Ontario, Canada M4V 3B2
Penguin Books (N.Z.) Ltd, 182–190 Wairau Road, Auckland 10, New Zealand

Penguin Books Ltd, Registered Offices: Harmondsworth, Middlesex, England

First published in the United States of America by Viking Penguin,
a division of Penguin Books USA Inc., 1991
Simultaneously published in Puffin Books
Published in a Puffin Easy-to-Read edition, 1993

5 7 9 10 8 6 4

Text copyright © Harriet Ziefert, 1991
Illustrations copyright © Mavis Smith, 1991
All rights reserved

LIBRARY OF CONGRESS CATALOGING-IN-PUBLICATION DATA
Ziefert, Harriet.
Harry gets ready for school / Harriet Ziefert;
pictures by Mavis Smith   p.   cm.—(Puffin easy-to-read) (Hello Reading!)
Summary: In preparation for his first day of school, Harry visits the doctor, dentist,
and barber, prepares pencils and a new outfit, and gets a good night's rest.
ISBN 0-14-036539-7
[1. Schools—Fiction. 2. Hippopotamus—Fiction.]
I. Smith, Mavis, ill. II. Title. III. Series.
IV. Series: Ziefert, Harriet. Hello reading!
[PZ7.Z487Haqn   1993]
[E]—dc20   93-16192   CIP   AC

Puffin® and Easy-to-Read® are registered trademarks of Penguin Books USA Inc.
Printed in the United States of America

Reading Level 1.7

Harry Gets Ready for School

Harriet Ziefert
Pictures by Mavis Smith

PUFFIN BOOKS

Everybody has a lot to do
before school starts.

And so does Harry.

A lot to do

A lot to do

A lot
A lot
A lot to do!

A checkup at the doctor

A checkup at the dentist

A barber is important, too.

Now Harry looks ready for school.

And school looks ready for Harry.

It's bedtime on the night
before school starts.

A lot to do

A lot to do

A lot
A lot
A lot to do!

Everybody's nervous on the night before school starts.

It's hard to sleep.

A little music helps Harry
fall asleep.

Sleep well, Harry.
Sleep well until…

it's morning on the day
school starts.

Turn off the clock.
Turn on the light.

Good morning, Harry.

A lot to do

A lot to do

A lot
A lot
A lot to do!

Hurry, Harry, or you'll miss the school bus.

Here's your lunch box.
Here's your backpack.

Good-bye, Harry.

Hello, school.

Hello, Harry.